Magic Gifts

*Some fairies on Sheepskerry Island
have a special gift for magic.
Like her sister Tinker Bell, Clara is
one of those fairies.*

So when Sheepskerry hosts the
Valentine's Games, Clara can't help
putting her magic to good use.
But fairy magic is a
powerful thing…

Other *Fairy Bell Sisters* stories:

The Fairy Bell Sisters

Hearts and Flowers for Clara

First published in the USA by HarperCollins Publishers Inc., in 2014
First published in Great Britain by HarperCollins *Children's Books* in 2014
HarperCollins *Children's Books* is a division of HarperCollins*Publishers* Ltd,
77-85 Fulham Palace Road, Hammersmith, London, W6 8JB.

The HarperCollins website address is: www.harpercollins.co.uk

1

Text copyright © Margaret McNamara 2014
Illustrations copyright © Erica-Jane Waters 2014

ISBN 978-0-00-752325-2

Margaret McNamara and Erica-Jane Waters assert the moral right to be
identified as the author and illustrator of this work.

Printed and bound in England by Clays Ltd, St Ives plc

For Donna Bell Bray

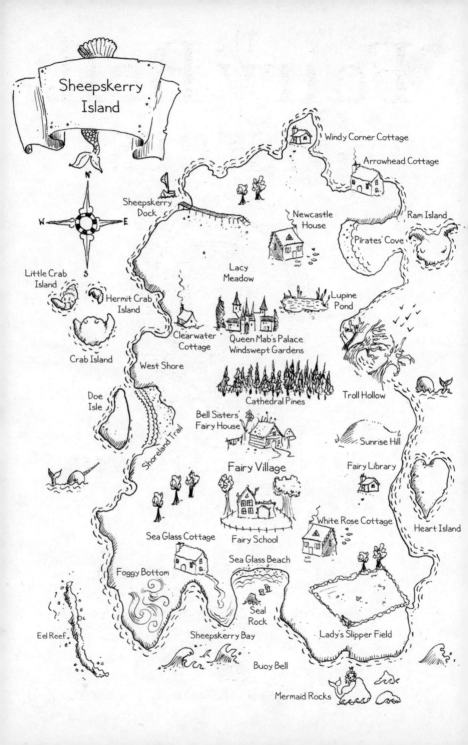

The Fairy Bell Sisters

Hearts and Flowers for Clara

Margaret McNamara

Illustrations by Erica-Jane Waters

HarperCollins *Children's Books*

 Chapter One

*V*alentine's Day for fairies is a lovely
affair, for fairies like to send and receive
valentines more than anything else.
(Anything else in February, that is.)
And Valentine's Week on Sheepskerry
Island is better than anywhere else,
because Queen Mab enchants Lady's
Slipper Field and turns the dark of
winter into the fresh breath of summer.
All the Sheepskerry fairies gather in the

meadow to exchange gifts and cards.
They smell the orange blossoms and
the roses. They throw off their heavy
coats and scarves and mittens and wear
their light summer dresses. They kick off
their shoes and turn their faces to the
warm sun.

Also, gnomes
come.

Gnomes?
You didn't
think there were
only *trolls* in the
world of the fairies,
did you? (Trolls
hibernate through the winter, by the
way.) Gnomes are terribly different from

trolls. Gnomes don't have warts, for one thing. They're not smelly. And they can talk properly, though they have a bit of a lilt to their speech as a result of living on the faraway Outer Islands. I know you may have seen garden gnomes with long beards and fishing poles, still as statues at the bottom of a garden. That's what gnomes look like when they get old and grumpy. But when they're young…

"When they're young, gnomes are lots of fun," said Clara Bell as she knotted a warm purple scarf round her neck. It was a very cold February day and all the Sheepskerry fairies were bundled up tightly, especially Tinker Bell's little sisters.

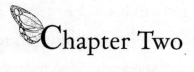

Chapter Two

I'm fairly certain you've met Tinker Bell's little sisters, but if you have not, let's please introduce them now. Here are:

Clara Bell

Lily Bell

Rosie Bell

Silver Bell

Squeak

The five Bell sisters – and their friend
Poppy Flower – were making their way
back from fairy school, which had let
out early today, as the snow was falling
fast and thick. They darted between
snowflakes as they flew.

"Gnomes *are* lots of fun," said Lily,
"even if too many of them wear those
awful pointy hats."

"I like their hats!" said Rosie.

"*Tutu!*" said Squeak.

"Me three!" said Silver. "And I don't mind what they wear as long as they're not too good at sports. Because I want to beat them all at the Valentine's Games."

That's another thing the fairies love about February: the Valentine's Games. I won't tell you about them now, as Rosie will tell us about them in a moment or two, if you can be patient.

"The only way you'd beat *all* the gnomes in your very first year of competition," said Lily, "is if you used magic, which unfortunately we don't have much of yet."

"Not true!" said Silver. "I've been training! Besides, I'll have lots of magic soon."

"Not too soon, I hope," said Rosie. "We still have some growing up to do before we get our magical powers." Rosie gave Silver a hug on the wing.

"But I'm sure when you do you'll be as magical as Tink herself."

That made Silver smile. And though none of her sisters saw it, Rosie's words made Clara smile too. She had been practising her fairy charms since her last birthday and she could already make a bell ring without touching it. (She was a Bell sister, after all!) Just last week, she'd taught herself how to make a rose bloom in the snow. Right now, she was working on her sparkle charm. That was a tricky one.

As Clara flew towards home, she thought about something that had happened long ago, when she was a very young fairy. She had noticed a tiny grasshopper in the tall grass near Lupine Pond. Its leg was broken, so it could not hop or even sing a grasshopper song to call for help. (Grasshoppers use their legs to make their songs!) Clara had known she didn't have a hope of helping the grasshopper – she hadn't even started learning charms yet at school. But she couldn't bear to see the injured insect. Then all at once, she recalled a charm she'd heard her big sister, Tinker Bell, recite once, long ago. How did it go?

Clear as crystal, Clara heard Tink's voice in her head. She closed her eyes, stretched out her arms, and said:

Harm and hurt
And pain no more.
Feel this power,
From my core.
May you be
Sound as a bell.
May my magic
Make you well!

Clara had felt faint and dizzy, and
it took a few moments before she was
well enough to open her eyes again.
She steadied herself and looked at the
grasshopper. It hadn't hopped away.
It was exactly where she had first
seen it. Her charm had failed!

But the very next moment she heard

18

a tiny little *chirrp* coming from her
grasshopper friend. That could only
mean…

"Your leg has healed!" she'd cried.

Then she'd heard a voice behind her.
"Clara. Clara Bell."

It was Queen Mab! Clara had nearly jumped out of her wings.

"Were you using magic?"

Clara almost had not dared to speak to the queen. But Queen Mab had asked her a question, and she could not let it go unanswered. "I was, Your Majesty," she'd said.

"The healing charm is very powerful, Clara Bell. Did you learn it from Tinker Bell?"

"I did, Queen Mab."

"Tink should know better than to teach that to you. It takes life to heal life."

Clara wasn't exactly sure what Queen Mab had meant when she said that. But she had curtsied deeply. "Forgive me, my queen," she'd said.

"Do not be ashamed, Clara Bell. You are a young fairy right now, but you have a gift for magic. You will be a very great fairy one day."

Clara could hardly believe her ears. "I will?" she'd asked in a whisper.

"Yes, Clara Bell, you will," said Queen Mab.

Clara had never forgotten that encounter with the queen. (Would you?) In fact, Queen Mab's words had given Clara great confidence her whole life.

However, I'd better warn you: if you're looking for a story where a very confident fairy sails along making clever decisions, always being careful, and never taking on more than she can manage, then this book will not be your cup of fairy tea. But if you'd like to hear about a fairy who's admired by all and expects so much of herself that she takes on far too much – so much that she almost risks her life – then you'll want to turn the page.

I'm keeping my fingers crossed you'll turn the page…

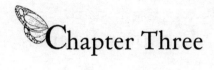 # Chapter Three

Phew! I can uncross my fingers!

# Chapter Four

*C*lara tucked the memory of Queen Mab's words into a pocket of her mind and flew in through the doorway of the Bell sisters' fairy house. She was thinking about her growing magic as the sisters sat around the fire together that evening.

"Rosie, I think you'd better finish your homework and stop writing that letter to Lulu," said Clara. "You're falling behind in Troll Tracks again."

"I just want to tell her about the Valentine's Games," said Rosie. Lulu was Rosie's friend – a real human child who believed in fairies (like someone else you might know). "I've written to her about the sack races and the long jump and the three-legged race and the tossing of the branches." She looked over her letter. It was already four pages long. "Now I need to tell her about the swim round the island. I hope the dolphins join in again."

"There's a baby dolphin this year," said Silver, who was trimming some lace. "Have you seen her? She's getting so fast! Poppy and I have named her Speedy."

25

"That's a cute name," said Lily.

"I know! Poppy wanted to name her Bluey but I told her my name was better."

"Bluey's nice too," said Rosie. "But whatever she's called, that little dolphin is the sweetest thing ever."

"*Coomada!*" said Squeak.

"Yes, we all love babies, don't we, Squeakie?" said Clara. She gave Squeak a big hug and looked over at Lily, who was deep in a pile of silk scarves. "How are Fairy Fractions going?"

"*Humph,*" said Lily.

"I love Fairy Fractions," said Silver. "Three-fifths of a starfish plus two-fifths of a starfish equals one whole starfish!"

"Very good," said Clara. "Lily, since you're not doing your homework, can you please get Squeakie into her pyjamas?"

"Not right now," said Lily. "I'm choosing a scarf to wear to the Games tomorrow." She picked one out from the pile. "This looks good with my sky-blue eyes, don't you think?" she asked the mirror, which did not reply. (Mirrors on Sheepskerry are not enchanted.)

Clara glanced at her sister and caught sight of her own reflection.

"You look nice tonight, Clara," said Silver. "Did you polish your wings?"

Clara had not polished her wings. She had not changed a thing about herself. And yet her long, dark hair was shinier than ever. Her skin almost glowed. And her eyes, always a deep brown, seemed to be flecked with gold.

Perhaps her newfound magic was giving her a glow from inside.

Chapter Five

"*O*h my word! The meadow is *gorgeous*!"

"Queen Mab has done her *best* magic
ever!"

The Fairy Bell sisters shook the
snow from their wings and flew into
Lady's Slipper Field. All the fairies were
gathering there. This year the enchanted
meadow was more lush and fragrant
and flower-filled than ever before.

"I think the gnomes must have done

some of this magical gardening," said Iris Flower. "It *is* their speciality."

"Off with this horrid winter hat!" Lily cried as she ran through the tall flowers. "Ooh! Avery!" she called to her best friend. "Can you feel that island sun?"

"Of course I can. It's a picture-perfect day!" said Avery.

"*I* must look picture perfect for when the gnomes arrive," said Lily. "How do you like my skirt?"

"It's pretty, Lily, but I don't think it will help you win any races," said Silver. "Heigh-ho, Poppy!" she called. "Let's do some flying practice. There's no snow to weigh our wings down here."

"I'll take Squeak out of her fairy
buggy," said Rosie. "She'll love being
barefoot again. We'll go for a romp,
won't we, Squeakie?" Rosie looked over
at her older sister. "Do you have time for
a quick walk, Clara?" she asked.

"No," said Clara. "I have too much work to do. I promised Queen Mab I'd organise the welcoming banquet and decorate the banqueting hall."

"You always take on so much," called Lily. "Queen Mab's lucky to have you."

"We're all lucky to have Clara," said Rosie.

What Rosie didn't know was that Clara actually wanted to be by herself. It was the perfect time to practise her sparkle charm. Most of the island would be deserted, as everybody would be in the meadow for the opening ceremony – which meant there would be not a soul on Sunrise Hill.

Clara darted out of the summery meadow and away up the hill. She hoped no one would notice where she was going.

It was cold and snowy up on the hill, but she knew the chilly wind wouldn't trouble her if she could get some magic going. She had studied her Fairy Charms book last night, after all her sisters had fallen asleep. If she did this charm just right, the top of Sunrise Hill would be transformed.

Clara had memorised the words of the charm – that wasn't the hard part. It was doing the arm movements properly and spinning at the correct speed so that she always ended up in the same spot. She closed her eyes and gave it a try:

Turn thrice around,
Fling wide your arm.
Sparkle now!
Obey my charm!

She opened her eyes – and started
coughing. The pretty white snow of
Sunrise Hill was covered in soot! "Where
did all – *ack* – this come from? *Ack! Ack!*"

Even the squirrels were covering their faces with their scrawny winter tails. "I must have done the spell all wrong!" Clara's eyes were streaming and her nose was running. "I'm so sorry, little squirrel," she said. "I'd better clear this soot before Queen Mab thinks there's been a fire on Sunrise Hill. Sparkles will drive the smoke away – but can I do it?"

Clara stood perfectly still and calmed her cough. She thought of what Queen Mab had said to her: *You will be a very great fairy one day.*

Clara filled her mind with the idea of her magical power. And she recited the charm again:

Turn thrice around,
Fling wide your arm.
Sparkle now!
Obey my charm!

Tentatively, Clara opened her eyes. The black soot was gone. In its place was a shimmering curtain of golden sparkles. The sparkles floated down to the ground and dusted the pure white snow, making it shine more brightly than Clara had ever seen. They landed on tree branches and turned the dark bark into patterns of shimmering gold. They turned the sweet little squirrel's coat golden, from whiskers to tail. The sparkles made Sunrise Hill, always a beautiful place, look absolutely breathtaking.

"I can't believe it!" cried Clara. "Oh, how beautiful! I did it! My first sparkle charm!"

A distant cheer went up from the meadow, and Clara remembered – the Welcoming Banquet. She hadn't done a thing to get ready!

# Chapter Six

Clara flew
from Sunrise
Hill back
to Queen
Mab's palace.
Everyone would
be arriving
there soon for
a hearty dinner.
She'd better get

going – fast.

"Hey, Clara!" It was Julia Jellicoe.
"You're going the wrong way!" Julia
flew right into Clara's path. "The opening
ceremony is almost over. Come on!"

"I'm not going, Julia," said Clara.
"I have too much work to do." Clara
hoped she didn't sound too prim. She
couldn't exactly tell Julia that she'd been
practising her magic. Not when she
hadn't mentioned it to her sisters – or
to Queen Mab. "I've got to set up the
Welcoming Banquet."

"Oh, thank goodness *somebody's*
going to organise it," said Julia. "There
are plates and dishes all over the place.
Ours is a surprise."

"Julia!" said Clara. "What kind of surprise?"

"The gnomes will love it. See you later!"

When Clara arrived at the palace, her cheeks were red and her toes were freezing. She flew into the banqueting hall and warmed up by the fire. Then she went into the kitchen and looked over the chart she had put up last week, just to make sure everyone had done their part.

"Oh dear me no!" she said. "They've done exactly what they said they wouldn't."

Welcoming Banquet Food Sign-up

Fairy Sisters	Dish
Jellicoe Sisters	~~Tomato Chutney~~ Jelly beans
Flower Sisters	~~Roasted broccoli florets~~ Poppy-seed cake
Seaside Sisters	~~Clam soup~~ Sea Salt Caramels
Cobweb Sisters	~~Tofu and carrots~~ Spun sugar
Oak Sisters	~~Acorn squash casserole~~ Chocolate nut clusters

Only two fairy families had brought
what they said they would:

Bakewell Sisters	Fairy cakes
Bell Sisters	Harmony Casserole

A single Harmony Casserole would
never feed an island of fairies plus a
colony of gnomes. And much as they
all liked sweets, the gnomes and fairies
would want something more filling after
spending all day outside. *What were they
all thinking?* Clara shook her head and
smiled a little. *At least we'll have some
great desserts.*

Since all Queen Mab's helpers were

at the meadow, any new cooking and preparing would be up to Clara. She looked in the queen's storeroom and was relieved (though not surprised) to see it was well stocked.

"This will be a challenge," said Clara. "But I think I'm up to it."

Clara set to work, humming to herself as she rolled up her sleeves and tied on an apron and started washing and sorting.

Before long, pots of water were boiling on the cooker, vegetables were scrubbed and eggs were beaten. Clara was putting the finishing touches on a pot of vegetable soup when she heard a long, joyous cheer from the meadow.

That will be the end of the opening ceremony, she thought. *They'll soon be here!*

She felt a gust of icy air come through the door.

"Rosie, is that you? I could really use some help. The fairies have only brought cookies and sweets, all because of those silly—"

"Gnomes?" said a deep voice.

Clara turned round. Oh no! A gnome was here – already!

"Hi. I'm Rowan."

"Oh, hello," said Clara.

Clara remembered Rowan from last year's Games. He had done such a good job! He'd taken fourth place among all the competitors. The two Grace sisters had won the second and third prizes. Only one other gnome – a young chap called Alasdair who'd come first – had done better than Rowan.

Clara wasn't sure what to say to Rowan. She hadn't ever really talked to a gnome before.

"Um, do you… do you remember who I am?" Rowan asked at last. "I was at the Games last year." He blushed. "You were in the, um… third row, second from the left when the Games began. You were giving out snacks to the fairies and explaining scoring to your sisters and looking after a little baby. All at the same time."

"Sounds like me."

"You're Clara Bell."

Clara's eyes widened. She wanted to reply, but she wasn't sure what to say. Rowan must have thought that meant she didn't remember who he was, because he added quickly, "I didn't win. I'm sure you remember that."

"You came in fourth," said Clara. "That's a pretty big honour."

"Not if you ask my big brother Alasdair."

"Alasdair's your big brother?" asked
Clara.

"Yes, and he never lets me forget
it," said Rowan. "He took first prize last
year. As usual. But I'm going to beat him
this year. I've been training all autumn."

"Training? What have you been
doing?"

Rowan told Clara all about how he'd
been practising for the Games – running
up his own island's steepest hill, lifting
boulders, swimming around the Outer
Islands.

"But I'm talking too much!" said
Rowan. "I'm sorry. Tell me about you,
Clara."

Clara hesitated. But she felt Rowan

would be very easy to talk to. Maybe
it was because she knew he'd soon go
back to the Outer Islands and she'd
never see him again. Maybe it was the
friendly twinkle in his dark eyes. "I've
been training too," she said.

"For the Games?" asked Rowan.

"No, my sister Silver has been training
for the Games. I've been training—"
Clara stopped herself. She wished
she had not brought it up. "Um, did
you know we have a baby dolphin in
Sheepskerry Bay?"

"Are you changing the subject?
Because I have a feeling I know
what you've been training for," said
Rowan. "I think you're coming into your

magic powers."

Clara was startled. How did he know?

"Gnomes can do one or two tricks when they're my age, but they don't get their full powers until they're much older," said Rowan. "Tell me what it's like."

Rowan was so friendly and Clara was so eager to talk about what was happening to her, that she found herself telling him all about her newfound magical powers. She even told him the story of the grasshopper… and what Queen Mab had said so many years ago.

"'A very great fairy'," said Rowan. "Now that is an honour."

"Maybe she says that to every fairy, just to give them confidence."

"But that wouldn't be true. Not every fairy becomes a truly great fairy. So I don't think it would be very queenly of her, would it?"

"I suppose not," said Clara. "But how did you guess that my powers were coming? Does it show somehow?"

Rowan busied himself stirring the soup Clara had made, though it didn't really need stirring. "You just look more grown-up than you did last year," he said. "Even prettier."

They heard a clatter behind them and Rosie burst through the door. "Clara! Julia Jellicoe told me what went on with

52

the banquet. Do you need some help?"

"We're almost all set, Rosie. Rowan here has been helping out." *And guessing things about me I thought nobody knew.* "If you two just finish up I'll decorate the banqueting hall."

"There's not a lot of time," said Rosie. "Everyone will be arriving in a minute."

"I've got a plan," said Clara.

Clara flew into the Banqueting Hall. The pine tables were scrubbed, the napkins were pressed and the tables were set for the welcoming banquet. It looked very simple and very plain.

"That's all very well for a colony of gnomes," said Clara to herself. "But for fairies… it lacks a certain sparkle."

Then she recited her charm.

Turn thrice around,
Fling wide your arm.
Sparkle now!
Obey my charm!

She spun round carefully and
opened her eyes, hoping for anything
but soot. "Oh my!" she cried.

The sparkle charm was different in the palace than it had been on the hill, but the effect was just as beautiful. Where there had been bare floors and empty vases, there were carpets of flowers and pots of blossoms. The tables had been covered with spun gold. Balloons and ribbons streamed from the ceiling and tiny glowing fairy lights sparkled like stars.

"Oh, it's gorgeous!" said Rosie when she flew in to see it. "How did you get all this done so quickly?"

"She works fast," said Rowan. Then he smiled at Clara. "Though it looks a bit like magic to me."

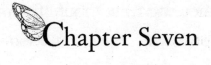

Chapter Seven

"*T*ug! TUG! T – U – G!"

Alasdair's team was winning the tug-of-war and Lily was almost out of her seat with excitement.

It was the morning after the Welcoming Banquet. Clara had saved the day.

"You were very smart to make us all some real food," Julia Jellicoe had told her. "Sorry we didn't bring

the tomatoes."

Clara smiled. The banquet had worked perfectly, even if it did wear her out more than she thought it would. There was piping-hot food (helped along by Rosie and Rowan) and everybody was thrilled with all the desserts. The dining hall itself was as magnificent as it had ever been – thanks to Clara's magic. Queen Mab had given Clara a warm smile when she saw the decorations. *Maybe she knows?* Clara thought.

Fairies and gnomes alike had enjoyed themselves

enormously. They'd all had a good
night's rest and now the Games were in
full swing.

"Come on, Alasdair! Win it for me!"
Lily cried.

With an enormous last PULL,
Alasdair's team of gnomes yanked the
other team across the centre line and
won the contest. "Hooray!" Lily cheered.
Alasdair waved at Lily in the stands. "I'm
fainting!" said Lily.

"You are such a goose!" said Silver.

"He doesn't really
care about you.
Look – now
he's waving at
Iris Flower."

Poppy, in the seat next to Silver, beamed. "I think he likes Iris too," she said.

"Alasdair is a little show-offy," said Rosie.

"He's not show-offy. He's just the best."

"We'll see about that, Lily," said Clara. "Alasdair is doing well, but the other gnomes are right behind him." She looked at the scoreboard. Alasdair was in first place; Rowan was a distant fifth. *Come on, Rowan*, she thought. *You can do it*.

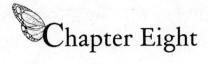# Chapter Eight

*A*ll that day, gnomes and fairies played
in the Valentine's Games together. The
fairies laughed and laughed as the
gnomes tried to sprint against them (of
course flying is faster than running!),
but the gnomes got their own back
when they competed in Tossing the
Branch. Twelve gnomes and fairies each
balanced a huge branch on the palms
of their hands and then tossed it as high

and far as they could. Alasdair was the winner of that contest too, but Rowan was a close second.

The most fun was the three-legged race. Queen Mab enchanted the leaves on the trees so that each one magically displayed the names of a pair of fairies or gnomes. When the queen said, "Leaves, fall upon us!" the green leaves on the enchanted trees of Lady's Slipper Field cascaded down.

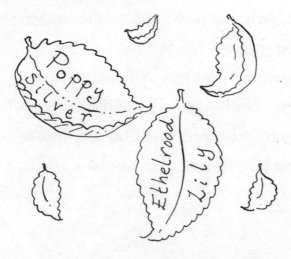

"I'm teaming up with… Poppy!" said Silver. "Queen Mab really knows what to do with her magic. I bet she thinks we'll win!"

"Don't be so sure, Poppy," said Clara. "These gnomes are awfully good."

"Look," said Lily, with a frown on her face, "my leaf says… Ethelrood." She wrinkled her nose as she looked at the scoreboard. "Ethelrood? What kind of a name is that? And he's in tenth place!"

"Ethelrood is a very old and respected gnomish name," said Clara.

"*Humph!*" said Lily.

Clara didn't want to look at the enchanted leaf that had fallen in her lap. *Maybe I'll be paired with Ro—*

"Clara!" Iris Flower exclaimed. "We're a team!"

She looked at her leaf. Sure enough, it bore the names *Clara* and *Iris*.

"We'll be a great team," she told her friend, and she meant it.

"Rosie got Squeakie!" cried Silver. "They're racing in the baby-buggy lanes with the other baby fairies and their big sisters. And Alasdair is partners with his brother." Silver paused. "What's his name – Owen."

"His name is Rowan," said Clara.

Queen Mab's clear voice rang out over Lady's Slipper Field. "Racers, prepare!"

"Come on, Silver!" called Poppy.

64

And with that, the meadow was fluttering with butterflies offering velvet ribbons to tie the racers' legs together.

"Grab a couple of ribbons, Poppy, but be careful of those butterflies' wings. We'll show those gnomes who can win a three-legged race!"

Queen Mab had changed the rules this year and paired some gnomes and fairies together, so the three-legged races, usually a competition of practised skill and coordination, turned into a bit of a dog's dinner. A mess, in other words.

There were three races and three prizes in all. In the first race, several fairy-and-gnome pairs ended up laughing so hard they never made it to

the finish line.
Including
Lily and
Ethelrood.
"He's
kind of
cute!" Avery
whispered to
Lily as they'd
passed her on
the sidelines.
In the second race, Rosie and Squeak
didn't even know whether they'd
crossed the finish line, but they had
such fun in the buggy lane that they
didn't care. And Clara and Iris, who
had been friends for such a long time,

ran swiftly together and came in a very respectable fourth, beating Andy and Hamish, two of the more popular gnomes.

Soon it was time for the last race.

"Line up!" cried Silver. "Line up, everybody!"

Rowan and Alasdair clomped down to the starting line. Silver and Poppy took their place next to them.

"Bet we beat you!" said Silver with a broad smile.

"May the best pair win!" said Rowan, smiling back. "And no flying!"

"We'll see who's best," said Alasdair. And with that, Lady Courtney, the queen's attendant, called "Ready…

67

steady… GO!" and they were off.

Clara watched, holding her breath, as the race started. She wanted to root for Rowan, but she had to cheer for her sister too. Poppy and Silver ran well together. Their legs were the same length; their stride was long; they even breathed together (and they didn't use their wings!). They pulled

ahead early and it was clear they were going to win until—

"No!" cried Clara. A branch caught Poppy's foot and she tumbled down, taking Silver with her.

Rowan and Alasdair raced ahead as Poppy and Silver sprang to their feet. They were just a short distance from the finish line.

The meadow rang with cheers. "Go, Alasdair!" cried the gnomes.

"Go, Silver! Go, Poppy, go!" cried the fairies.

As if they were one fairy, Silver and Poppy got back on track, hit their stride and raced towards the finish line.

The roar from the crowd was tremendous. "You can do it, fairies! You can do it!"

With one last surge of strength, Silver and Poppy crossed the finish line... just one wing's width in front of Alasdair and Rowan.

"Hooray!" cried the fairies and they flapped their wings for joy.

"Well done, Poppy," said Rowan,

when he caught his breath. "And you too, Silver. Are you all right? That was quite a fall you took."

"Ha!" said Silver. "That was nothing."

"We still got fifteen points!" said Alasdair.

"But you beat us fair and square," said Rowan. Then he looked around at the crowd. "You're… um, Clara's sister, aren't you?"

"Yes," said Silver. "I'm the youngest Bell sister, except for baby Squeak."

"You sisters really get along well together, don't you?"

"Of course we do!" Silver laughed. "Except when Lily teases me too much. Then we're glad to have Clara there – she takes care of us all."

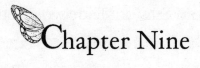

Chapter Nine

*L*ater that afternoon, as the other gnomes and fairies enjoyed an enchanted snack (fairy doughnut holes!), Clara flew away from the sunny meadow. The competitions were over for the day and there'd be just enough time for her to try out some more magic.

Clara set her wings eastwards and made the long flight up to Sunrise Hill. It was very cold out, but she loved the sting of the wind on her cheeks. It made her feel so alive – as if there was nothing she couldn't do.

An elegant mother deer crossed Clara's path and looked at her curiously with its big brown eyes. Clara flew over to her and gently touched the tip of her nose. Deer are very friendly on Sheepskerry and Clara knew this doe from last year's harsh winter, when she had helped the mother deer find

delicious beechnuts to eat. "Do you
need some more food to eat, Doe-deer?"
asked Clara. "I wish I could magic some
up for you."

The sound of trampling startled them
both and the mother deer bounded
away. Clara turned quickly. Maybe it
was a bear!

But it wasn't a bear at all.

"Rowan!" Clara said.

Rowan Gnome stood in front of
Clara. Gnomes cannot fly, of course, so
Rowan had clamped on his ice shoes
and taken the slippery path to the top
of the hill. Fairies don't mind if the
paths are slippery and slick, because
they don't need to use them much. (You

wouldn't walk on ice, either, if you had wings.)

"What are you doing up here?" asked Clara. She always thought of Sunrise Hill as her own special place, especially when fluffy snowflakes were falling, as they were that afternoon.

"The other gnomes told me about Sunrise Hill. They say it's the highest place on Sheepskerry. That's why I brought my sledge."

"Ooh, that's a beautiful one," said Clara. "We hardly ever do any sledging on Sheepskerry. Most fairies prefer to fly."

"This hill is perfect for a sledge ride," said Rowan. "And this snow is perfect...

for snowballs."

"Don't you dare," said Clara.

"Oh, I wouldn't think of it," said
Rowan. He whistled innocently. "But I
may pile up a little snow here, just in
case."

Clara beat him to it. She scooped
up a handful of snow, smushed it into
a ball, took aim – and threw! *Ploop!*
Clara's snowball
landed on
Rowan's
shoulder.

"Why, you…"
said Rowan.
He grinned. "I
knew I couldn't

trust you." He made an armful of white powder into a big ball. "Watch out, Miss Fairy."

"Can't catch me!" said Clara. "I can fly!"

"Not fair!" said Rowan.

Clara had speed and grace, but Rowan had an excellent throwing arm. After Clara dodged several well-aimed tosses and Rowan's cap got knocked off a third time (cue a lot of laughing), they called a truce.

"Want to build a snow gnome?" asked Rowan.

"No thanks!" said Clara, her eyes merry. "I'll build a snow fairy."

The two of them got to work rolling snow and sculpting faces. Rowan went off looking for a pinecone for a pipe. "You have lots of interesting stones on Sheepskerry," he said, picking one up and putting it in his pocket.

"And sea glass too," said Clara. "Just ask Lily about her collection. Have you found the right pinecone yet? I'm using twigs for fairy wings."

They worked for a while longer as the snow fell. Soon there was a sturdy snow gnome and a beautiful snow fairy on the top of Sunrise Hill.

"She needs a scarf to keep her warm," said Clara, looking at her fairy. "I'll give her mine." She unwound her purple scarf from her neck

and wrapped it round her snow fairy.
"Much better," she said.

"My gnome needs a cap, but he's not
getting mine, not after I had to rescue
it from your snowballs so many times."
Rowan looked around him. "Plus, the
snow is coming down harder now."

All at once, Clara realised she'd been
having so much fun that she hadn't
even thought about Rosie and Lily, Silver
and Squeak. "I'd better get home," said
Clara. "What if my sisters need me? They
won't even know where I am!"

"We'll send them word, to let them
know you're all right," said Rowan.
He whistled a low whistle and the doe
Clara had seen earlier came bounding

through the snow.

"You can talk to deer?" asked Clara in wonder.

"Oh, it's not much of a skill. All of us gnomes can talk to woodland creatures," said Rowan. He cradled the deer's neck in his arms, very gently, and whispered in her ear. The doe bounded off again. "She'll tell Queen Mab. Your sisters will be fine."

"Let's hope so," said Clara. "I worry about them." And she started to fly away.

"Wait, Clara," said Rowan. "Your wings might get bogged down in this snow. Come on the sledge with me. It'll be the quickest way."

Much as she wanted to fly, Clara knew Rowan was right. She climbed on to the long, slender sledge behind him. Suddenly cold, she shivered.

"Here," said Rowan. "Take my scarf."

Clara was too chilled to turn him down. He knotted his old brown knitted scarf round her neck.

"Thanks, Rowan," she said.

"Oh," he said, "it's nothing." He paused for a moment. "Will you be all right?" he asked.

"I'll be fine," she said.

"Then hold on tight!" he said. "Let's go!"

Chapter Ten

*S*wiftly, they raced down Sunrise Hill. Clara laughed as they bumped and slipped and slid their way down the hill. "I've never gone this fast on land before!" she called, her eyes bright. She would have enjoyed the ride even more if she hadn't been so worried about her sisters. When they reached the deep snow at the bottom of the hill, Clara said a hasty goodbye to Rowan. Then she flew towards home.

Under the cover of trees, Clara did not need to worry about snow on her wings. She flew straight to the Bell fairy house. All the way home, she fretted about what she would find there: Rosie overwhelmed, Lily in tears, Silver frozen in a snowbank and Squeak crying her eyes out, frightened and alone. Why couldn't she fly any faster?

Finally, panting and out of breath, she arrived at her beloved fairy house. She burst through the door. "Oh, sisters, sisters, where are you? Are you safe? Are you all right?"

She looked around. She didn't see anyone. Not even Rosie. Not even Squeak!

"Lily, Silver – where are you?" she cried. "Rosie! Squeakie! Have I lost you forever?" Then Clara heard a very familiar sound.

"*No lolo!*"

In front of the fire, in a cosy heap, were Rosie, Lily, Silver and Squeak. Three mugs of steaming hot chocolate were on the toadstool table (plus a

special bottle of warm milk for you-know-who). Fluffy white marshmallows were roasting on sticks. The

smell of popcorn was in the air. The
great room was as warm as toast.

"You're all right?" Clara said. "You
knew what to do without me?"

"Of course we're all right," said Rosie.
"We've had so much fun! This house is
toasty warm too."

"Doesn't Sheepskerry look pretty?"
asked Lily. "Everything's white and
fresh."

"Queen Mab herself flew over to see
us," said Silver. "She got a message from
a deer!"

"Where were you all this time?" asked
Lily.

Clara hesitated a little. Then she said,
"I was up on the top of Sunrise Hill with

Alasdair's brother. Rowan."

"Rowan!" said Silver. "What were you doing all that time with a gnome?"

"Chatting about the Games, I'm sure," said Rosie. She noticed the new scarf round Clara's neck. "He seems like a nice gnome," she said to her big sister.

"He is," said Clara. "I really think he is."

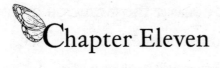 Chapter Eleven

"*T*he Round-the-Island Swim begins...
now!"

All the fairies cheered as Alasdair,
Rowan, Hamish, Cam, Andy, Ethelrood
and the other gnomes dived off the
dock and splashed into Sheepskerry
Bay early the next morning. The fairies
didn't generally participate in this race –
it wasn't wise to take off their wings for
such a long time.

"It must be freezing in that water!" said Silver. "How do they do it?"

"Queen Mab enchanted the bay," said Rosie. "She made the water as warm as it is in summertime."

"Even then it's too cold for me," said Lily, with a shiver.

"Still, I'd like to try a Round-the-Island Swim sometime. I could do it so fast my wings wouldn't even notice they were off my shoulders," said Silver. "Maybe next year!"

"It's all riding on this!" Lady Courtney announced. "If Alasdair wins, he takes first prize. But since this event is such a high-scoring one, Rowan or Ethelrood could snatch the trophy away from him.

What will be the outcome? Who will win the Valentine's Games?"

All the fairies were crowded at the dock to watch the beginning of the race. They started flying towards the West Shore to follow the gnomes' progress when they heard a shout from Iris Flower.

"Come on, everybody," she called. "Queen Mab sent the Royal Balloon so we can follow the race! It's waiting for us behind Clearwater Cottage! Come on!"

Queen Mab hardly ever brought out the Royal Balloon, but when there was going to be a traffic jam of fairies in the sky, it was the best solution.

The Royal Balloon wasn't really a balloon, but everybody called it that. It was an intricate straw basket, lined with deep blue velvet, that was pulled by a flock of very friendly birds who lived on Sheepskerry all year round. The black-capped birds chittered with excitement as the fairies piled in.

"Come on, Silver!" cried Poppy. "Climb aboard!" Next, her own sisters disappeared into the basket. She heard Rosie calling. "Clara! Clara, where are you?"

Clara almost floated over to the balloon to be with her friends... but then she thought, *They'll be able to see the whole race from up there, but if I stay closer to shore, I can follow Rowan.* "Go ahead!" she called to Rosie. "Go ahead without me!"

The birds whistled to one another and they lifted the balloon gently into the sky. The fairies could soon spot their favourites.

"Come on, Alasdair," cried Lily. "He's winning!"

"Is that Ethelrood right behind him?" asked Avery. "He's in second place."

"Where's Andy?" asked Julia Jellicoe.

"I hope they all win!" said Rosie.

"*A-blay*!" said Squeak.

"Yes, Squeakie," said Rosie. "Hooray!"

Clara did not feel sorry that she wasn't up in the balloon with the other

94

fairies. She was enjoying the race along the shoreline. The pack of swimmers had just passed Little Crab Island and was heading south to Doe Isle.

There was an old-fashioned loudspeaker in the balloon's basket and Lady Courtney used it now. "It's Alasdair in the lead," she announced, "with Ethelrood just behind. Andy and Hamish are going strong. Rowan lags, but his stroke is steady."

"Go, Ethelrood!" called Avery.

"And look, fairies! The school of dolphins is helping them along. Nothing more exciting than to try to outswim a dolphin."

"There's Speedy!" called Silver.

Climbing over the rocks near Sea Glass Cottage, Clara was urging Rowan on. "Alasdair has pulled out ahead early," she said to a pretty mother gull she met on the path, "but I have a feeling Rowan will outpace him."

And indeed Clara was right. As the swimmers rounded Foggy Bottom, Alasdair's fast pace flagged and Rowan, who had been slow but steady, began to pull ahead. "Go, Rowan, go!" called Clara.

But then the race slowed down.

"What's this?" said Lady Courtney through her loudspeaker. "Are those… mermaids in the water? They promised Queen Mab they would not disturb the swimmers!"

"We don't always keep our promises!" sang the mermaids. *"Surely you know that by now."*

Clara watched as the mermaids swirled around the gnomes, making them lose their way in the water. Even the dolphins lost their formation as the mermaids splashed and dashed and kicked. *"Over this way!"* they sang. *"No, here!"* They held out charms made of pearls and coral to lure the gnomes off course and cause all kinds of mischief, all the way from Eel Reef to Mermaid Rocks.

Soon, most of the swimmers had gone astray. Hamish was heading back to Doe Isle and Cam was swimming out to sea. Alasdair joined the three prettiest mermaids on Seal Rock and rested for a while. "I'm still going to win," he called to the fairies in the Royal Balloon. "But how can I resist a mermaid?"

The one gnome who was not bothered by the mermaids was Rowan. His strong, steady stroke took him easily past Mermaid Rocks, towards the sand beds of Heart Island. Clara was sure he would win the race – and take the gold prize. But then he too stopped swimming suddenly and started treading water.

"What is he doing?" Clara said as she strained her eyes to watch him from the

shore. "Have the mermaids enchanted him too?"

Rowan didn't appear to be hurt or tired, but he wasn't moving one bit. And now that the mermaids had grown bored with them, the other gnomes were once again on course.

"And the race is back on!" cried
Lady Courtney from the Royal Balloon.
The fairies whistled and cheered as the
swimmers headed north to Ram Island.
The Royal Balloon was all but out of
sight.

Clara stayed where she was. She
could see that Rowan was panting hard
in the water. He was swimming over to
rest on a shoal. He didn't look hurt or
injured, but she couldn't be sure. And
he seemed to be dragging something
with him. "Shall I fly out to help him,
little fellow?" asked Clara as a chipmunk
scampered up a chestnut tree. "Do you
think he needs me?"

The chipmunk ran halfway up the

tree and pointed his nose to precisely where Rowan was in the water.

That was good enough for Clara. She gave a few strong flaps of her wings and took flight to the spot where Rowan had stopped swimming. It was cold out in the bay, but Clara bravely faced the wind. As she got closer to Rowan he waved to her, but without his familiar smile.

"What's wrong, Rowan? Are you hurt?"

Then Clara realised why Rowan had stopped. There, in front of them, was a baby dolphin, caught on the sand beds of Heart Island. "Oh no! It's Speedy!" cried Clara. "She's lost her way. Let's

take her back to her pod." Clara landed
carefully on the slippery rock where
Rowan held the dolphin in his arms.

"It's not as easy as that, Clara,"
Rowan said. "This little dolphin is hurt.

Take a look at her flank."

There was a deep gash on the baby
dolphin's side. "She must have cut herself
on these sharp rocks," Clara said. "Can
you call the mother dolphin? The way
you called the doe?"

"I already have," said Rowan. "But
creatures of the sea don't always
understand gnomes. I don't think she
could hear me."

"Shall I fly off to get Queen Mab? Her
magic could help us."

Speedy's body shivered.

"There's no time," said Rowan.

"Then I'll have to do it," said Clara.
"I'll have to try the healing charm." She
didn't want to repeat what Queen Mab

103

had said: *It takes life to heal life.*

"Will it not take too much out of you?" asked Rowan. "You told me it's not an easy charm."

Speedy made a tiny sighing sound. Her eyes fluttered. Clara could not just stand by and do nothing. Not when there was a chance she might save the baby dolphin.

"I've got to do it, Rowan," she said. "I've got to try the healing charm."

She could not bring herself to say, *even if it costs me dearly, very dearly indeed.*

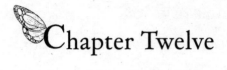

Chapter Twelve

*R*owan closed his eyes. Clara did too. They both put their hands on the baby dolphin. "Now, imagine her all well and safe," said Clara. She thought hard about Speedy swimming away to safety, healthy and free. Then she whispered the charm:

> *Harm and hurt*
> *And pain no more.*

Feel this power,
From my core.
May you be
Sound as a bell.
May my magic
Make you well!

Before Clara could even open her eyes, she heard the raspy breath of the baby dolphin again. She looked down at Speedy's side – the cut was still there. Her charm had failed!

"Why won't it work when it worked before? It's so much more important now," Clara said.

"It's OK, Clara," said Rowan. "You can't do everything. The mother dolphin

will be here soon, I'm sure." But he did
not sound so sure.

They both looked at the baby
dolphin. Her eyes were closing. "We're
losing her!" cried Clara. "I've got to try it
again."

Clara held out her hand and Rowan
took hold of it. "Now," she said,
"think of Speedy, safe and healed and
swimming back to her pod. Think hard,
Rowan!" He squeezed her hand and then
let her go.

Clara raised her arms and felt her
magic surge through her. Loud and clear
she said:

Harm and hurt
And pain no more.
Feel this power,
From my core.

May you be
Sound as a bell.
May my magic
Make you well!

Suddenly, magical sparks flew all around them.

"She's breathing, Clara! She's alive!"

Clara looked down at Speedy's side. The cut had healed without a trace and her tail flicked. She took a deep breath. "She's full of life!" Clara said in a hoarse whisper.

"We did it, Rowan. We saved her."

"You saved her," said Rowan.

And as if she could understand their language, the baby dolphin did a flip off the shallow sand beds and made a dive into the deep water. Then she came up again with a big dolphin grin on her face. Her mother and her aunties in the dolphin pod had found her and come to claim her. All at once, the pod of dolphins skittered on their tails out of the water as a way of saying thank you to Rowan and especially to Clara.

"We're so happy we could help you," Rowan called to them. "Aren't we, Clara?"

But when Rowan turned to Clara,

he saw that all the colour had drained from her face.

"What is it, Clara?" asked Rowan.

Clara's wings were white as sheets. Her head hung down. She was trembling all over.

"Clara, what's wrong?"

Clara could only speak in a whisper. "Queen Mab told me, 'It takes life to heal life.' Now I understand what she meant."

"No!" cried Rowan. "Clara! We've got to get you home!"

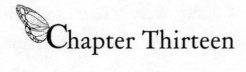# Chapter Thirteen

*R*owan Gnome was out on a rock in the middle of Sheepskerry Bay with a very ill fairy who had to get to safety. If he plunged into the water with Clara, she might be too weak to get to shore. If he left her there to get help, something terrible might happen before anyone could come to her aid.

"Go, Rowan," said Clara in a low voice. "Leave me here and get some help.

It's all you can do. Oh, and your race—"

"That's not important now," said Rowan. "I'm not leaving your side."

The dolphin pod circled around them. Speedy nuzzled Rowan with her nose. "Not now, Speedy!" said Rowan. "Clara already helped you. She needs help now."

Speedy tried again. This time, she made a little squeaking noise. The other dolphins joined in.

"What is it, dolphins?" said Rowan. "What do you want?"

Then all at once it was clear to him. *Come and ride on our backs*, they seemed to say. *Clara helped us. Now we'll help Clara.*

In a moment, the strongest mother dolphin circled the rock where Clara lay. Rowan climbed on to the dolphin's back and pulled Clara tight behind him.

He paused for a moment. "Will you be all right?" he asked.

This time, she could barely say the words. "I'll be fine."

"Then hold on tight!" he said. "Let's go!"

And through the water they glided towards Sheepskerry.

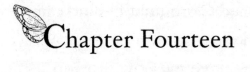# Chapter Fourteen

Of course by now, the Fairy Bell
sisters had spotted their big sister out in
Sheepskerry Bay. The birds carrying the
Royal Balloon spun round and dropped
down to where Clara was riding on the
dolphin's back. The mermaids saw them
coming and for once made no mischief.
In fact, they reached their arms up to
steady the basket of fairies.

"Here she is!" called Rowan.

The Royal Balloon hovered just centimetres above the water. Rowan was almost forgotten as Rosie, Lily, Silver, and even baby Squeak helped Clara into the basket.

"They have me now, Rowan," said Clara. "I'll be all right. You could even finish the race if you want."

"The race!" said Rowan.

"Don't use up your strength talking," said Lily. "Take us *home*!"

"To Queen Mab's palace, quickly, birds!" called Lady Courtney. "There's no time to lose!"

"She'll be better off at the palace, Lily," said Rosie. She was cradling Clara's pale face in her hands. "Queen

Mab will know what to do."

"Please go quickly, *please*!" said
Silver. "I'll do everything right from now
on, I promise. Just please get Clara
better again."

"*Jojo!*" said Squeak.

And like lightning, the birds flew
Clara away.

Chapter Fifteen

I don't want to keep you in suspense about Clara for too long. I'd like to say that she recovered her strength in the Royal Balloon. Or that she was better once she landed on Sheepskerry soil. Or even when she first arrived at Queen Mab's palace.

But none of that would be true.

Instead, Clara could barely lift her head to thank the birds who flew so fast. She could not manage to smile at Lady Courtney, who carried her through Queen Mab's palace towards one of the inner chambers. She could not even summon the strength to squeeze her sisters' hands when they clustered around her, hoping she might show some signs of recovery. And she did not see Rowan, who retired from the swimming race and paced back and forth in the Great Hall of the palace, waiting for news.

"Shall we send for Tink?" Rosie asked Queen Mab.

"Tink cannot do anything for Clara now," said Queen Mab. "Clara will have to draw strength from within to heal

119

herself. I will do my utmost to help her."
Then she added gently, "Sing her a song
so she knows you're outside." And she
turned towards Clara's chamber.

Rosie, Lily and Silver lifted their
voices in song and Squeak swayed in
rhythm:

> *Let the circle be unbroken,*
> *As we wait here, by her side.*
> *Let the circle be unbroken,*
> *We'll abide here, we'll abide.*

Queen Mab flew silently into the
chamber.

"Dear Clara Bell, you used too
much magic, too soon, to help another

creature in need. Now you are the one who must heal."

Clara was able to lift her head, just a little. "Do you think I can do it?" she asked.

"I know you can," said Queen Mab. "You will be a very great fairy some day."

Clara turned her head away.

"Or have you forgotten my words?" said Queen Mab.

Clara managed a very small smile. "Never, my queen. Never."

"Then draw from your strength within, Clara Bell. And heal."

Queen Mab raised her arms and the room was filled with light. She kneeled

down at Clara's bedside. Then, slowly
and carefully, in a deep strong voice,
she said:

> *Harm and hurt*
> *And pain no more.*
> *Strength be with you,*
> *From your core.*

> *For you, Clara,*
> *Do I kneel.*
> *May <u>your</u> magic*
> *Make you heal!*

Clara's eyes blinked. Her cheeks
flushed with colour.

"Come, fairies!" called Queen Mab to

the Fairy Bell sisters. "Come and help your sister."

Rosie, Lily, Silver and Squeak rushed into the bedchamber.

"You can do it, Clara!"

"You're getting better, I can see it!"

"Coomada, coomada!"

"We love you, Clara! We love you!"

Outside the palace, the fairies and gnomes waiting for news heard a magnificent cheer. Then the windows to the bedchamber were flung open.

"She's all better!" cried Rosie.

"She's smiling!" cried Lily.

"She did it!" cried Silver.

"*A-blay!*" cried Squeak.

And down in the Great Hall, Rowan Gnome rubbed his eyes and blew his nose into his gnomish handkerchief. He would tell anyone who asked that his allergies were acting up, but if you ask me, I'd say there might be another reason why his eyes had welled with tears.

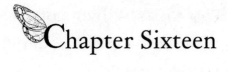

Chapter Sixteen

*C*lara had never been as happy as she was at the Farewell Banquet that night. She felt as healthy as she had ever felt in her life – lighter and fuller of life. Queen Mab took care of all the arrangements for the banquet this time, and the feast was delicious. There was a roaring fire in the hearth and all the gnomes and fairies were dressed in their cosiest winter jumpers. Everyone was delighted to be there and the faces of the Fairy Bell sisters were pink with joy. Tink sent Clara a 'get well' card that appeared in the middle of the feast by magic.

"Look!" said Rosie. "The postmark is *Neverland!*"

Inside there was a very special message:

> *I know you'll already be better when you get this, Clara. Queen Mab was right about you!*
> *Hugs and kisses,*
> *Tink*

Everything would have been perfect, except that Rowan was nowhere to be seen. His friends Cam and Hamish told Clara he'd get there after the banquet. "He's working on a little project," said Cam. "He'll be along soon."

When supper was finished, the insect orchestra played a fanfare and Queen Mab flew up to the palace stage.

"These have been some wonderful Valentine's Games," said Queen Mab. "Fairies and gnomes competed together in our annual contest. Silver Bell broke the record in Fairy Flight." She looked at Silver and Silver beamed. "And another record was set in Tossing the Branch, thanks to Alasdair Gnome." Alasdair flexed his muscles and flashed a grin at Iris Flower. "And as to the dramatic

ending to the Games and Clara Bell's
magnificent rescue –" Clara wished
Rowan were there with her – "we will
speak of that in a moment.

"Now," said Queen Mab, "Lady
Courtney will help me award the prizes
to the top three winners. But before I do,
let me say this to our gnomish friends:
it is a great honour to have had you
here on Sheepskerry. You all showed
most impressive skills. We look forward

to welcoming you
back to next year's
Valentine's Games!"

A great roar went
up from the crowd.
Lady Courtney

hovered next to Queen Mab. "May I begin?" she asked.

"Please do," said the queen.

"In third place," Lady Courtney announced, "is Ethelrood Gnome, with seventy-four points!" The fairies fluttered their wings and the gnomes cheered loud and long.

"He's awfully nice," said Avery.

"Alasdair's taller," said Lily.

"Ethelrood Gnome," said Queen Mab. "You have performed honourably and well. Please come forward and accept your prize."

The Stitch sisters had made the prizes for the Games again this year. They had crafted a gorgeous quilted vest for

third place, the colour of a bronze bell.
Ethelrood put on the vest with pride. "I
dedicate my win to… Avery Pastel!" said
Ethelrood.

Cheers and hoots came from the
gnomes. Avery flew up to Ethelrood,
who was smiling broadly. "Nice work,
Ethelrood," she said with a shy smile.

"You can call me Roody," said
Ethelrood with a grin. "And thanks for
thinking I'm cute. I think you're cute
too."

"In second place," said Lady
Courtney, "is Silver Bell, with eighty-five
points!"

The cheers began again. Silver flew
up to the stage.

"Here is your prizewinner's cape for second place," she said. And she handed Silver a forest-green cape shot with silver thread. "An extraordinary achievement for your very first competition."

"Thank you, Queen Mab!" she said. "And I bet you know who I dedicate my Games to: my big sister Clara!" said Silver.

Clara beamed with pride.

"And in first place," said Lady Courtney in her loud, clear voice, "with ninety-six points…"

Iris Flower sighed out loud.

"Gnomes and fairies, please stand for Alasdair Gnome!"

"Hooray for Alasdair!" they cried.

"Hooray for Alasdair Gnome!"

Alasdair climbed on to the podium. "Thank you, thank you," he said. Then he asked, "Where's my little brother, Rowan? Where's Rowan Gnome?"

"Hey, Rowan," said Hamish. "Get up front!"

1

Rowan was all the way at the back of the banqueting hall. His friends pushed him forward.

"There you are, Rowan," said Alasdair. "I wanted you to be here to hear me say... I dedicate my first-place win to my brother, Rowan. The bravest gnome in all the land!"

A huge cheer went up from the crowd. The Fairy Bell sisters cheered loudest of all.

Clara flew over to talk to Rowan.

"I'm sorry you gave up your chance of winning for me, Rowan," she said. "You could have beaten Alasdair, you know."

"That's water under the bridge – or

under the dolphin," said Rowan and he grinned. "Maybe next year."

Queen Mab cleared her throat and the crowd was quiet. "Which leads me to my final announcement," she said. "All of you know of the daring and selfless rescue Clara Bell performed during the Round-the-Island Swim. What many of you do not know is that Clara Bell has come into her magical powers."

There was a murmur of "ooh"s and "aah"s and some "I told you so"s throughout the crowd.

"Clara has powers that I did not realise she would have this early," said Queen Mab. "She achieved something remarkable out in Sheepskerry Bay. It

134

took some life from her, but she restored that life to herself. Rowan Gnome was a hero too, for getting Clara back to Sheepskerry and safety. Rowan, please come up and take a bow."

The crowd cheered again and Cam and Andy whistled.

"And Clara Dawn Bell, please come and take your place next to me. You are now a truly magical fairy."

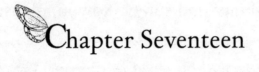Chapter Seventeen

At first, some fairies thought Clara had
not come into her magical powers that
night. For Clara's dress did not transform
into a golden gown; her hair did not
spin into curls; her arms and throat did
not shine with jewels. But those who
know Sheepskerry, and the fairies who
live there, realised that Clara was indeed
an enchanted fairy, even if she didn't
change on the outside. As she flew up

to the stage to take her place next to
Rowan, her wings were strong, her path
was steady, her eyes sparkled, her smile
beamed and there was a glow about her
that comes from magic alone.

Rowan and Clara danced
the first dance of the
Farewell Banquet
together. And they
danced all the other
dances of the evening
together too.

At the end of that
beautiful night, as the
tide was turning, the
gnomes boarded their boats
and said goodbye to the Sheepskerry

137

fairies. As Alasdair chatted loudly (he was asking *all* the fairies for their snail mail addresses) and Ethelrood smiled at Avery, Rowan walked with Clara under the moonlight on Sheepskerry Dock.

"I have something for you," he said. "It's why I was late to the banquet."

Clara looked at what Rowan held out
to her.

"It's… it's a valentine's gift," he said.

Indeed it was a valentine's gift of
sorts, but it wasn't made of shiny paper
or delicate lace. It was made of stone.

"This is the stone I found on Sunrise
Hill," said Rowan. "It's in the shape
of—"

Clara took it from him gently. "It's in
the shape of a heart," she said.

"I painted it myself," said Rowan,
blushing again. "Fairies like pink. At
least that's what Hamish and Cam told
me."

Clara smiled at the splash of pink
on the stone heart. Rowan was a better

swimmer than he was a painter.

"Look at the back," said Rowan.

Clara turned it over. Carved into the stone were two little words:

YOU ROCK

"Get it?" said Rowan. "It's a rock and— "

"I get it," said Clara. "And Rowan?" She smiled. "You rock too."

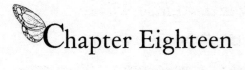

Chapter Eighteen

"*H*ere's another one for you, Clara!" said Silver.

The next morning, the Fairy Bell sisters were opening their valentine's cards over a breakfast of mint tea, crumpets, Cheshire cheese and grapefruit marmalade. Clara opened the pretty pink envelope and took out a handmade card from Silver.

"Don't you love it?" asked Silver.

"I do," said Clara. She read it aloud:

Roses are red
Violets are blue
Be careful with magic
Whatever you do!
With lots of hugs on Valentine's
Day from your little sister Silver.

"Oh, Clara will be careful with her magic," said Rosie. "But you are growing up, aren't you, Clara?"

"It's fine if you grow up," said Lily. "But you'd better not move away from us for a long, long time. Who would help me with my fractions?"

"And who would I have to share my secrets with?" said Rosie.

"And who'd keep me from getting in too much trouble?" said Silver.

"*Squeak*!" said Squeak.

They all looked at Clara. "You're not going to leave us, are you, Clara?" asked Silver.

"I'll tell you one thing," said Clara,

"nobody's going anywhere until these breakfast dishes are done." She grinned. "Silver, you clear the plates. I'll wash them and Lily can dry."

"Or they can air-dry," said Lily.

"And Rosie, you'll get Squeakie into her snowsuit, won't you?"

"I certainly will," said Rosie.

The sisters bustled about and soon all their work was done. They put on boots and hats and gathered up their valentine's gifts and cards to deliver to their fairy friends. Of course Silver could only find one of her mittens. "I have an extra pair upstairs," said Clara. "I'll be right back."

Clara flew upstairs and quickly found

a pair of warm mittens to fit Silver.
Before she went downstairs again,
she opened up the top drawer of her
cupboard. In it was the very special
valentine's gift Rowan had given her,
wrapped in an old brown scarf. She
took it out carefully. The pink paint was
already flaking off, but nothing would
change the shape of the heart-shaped
rock or what Rowan had written in
the stone.

YOU ROCK

"Clara! What are you doing up there?"
called Lily from downstairs. "We can't
wait forever."

Clara smiled. "But maybe I will,"
she said as she put Rowan's heart

back where it belonged. "Coming!" she
called to her sisters.

She flew down the stairs, linked arms
with Rosie and opened the door to the
dazzling day.

FAIRY SECRETS

Squeak's Words

A-blay! – Hooray!

Coomada – Love it!

Jojo! – Hurry!

No lolo – Don't be sad.

O-bee! – Not me!

Tsk-tsk – Do it!

Tutu! – Me too!

Squeak! – Oops! or Uh-oh! or
Yay! or sometimes, *Yikes!*

How to Make Stone Valentine's Gifts

These directions can be used by fairies, gnomes or children.

Look in your garden or a park or even on a beach for stones.

- Stones that are oval
- or round
- or heart-shaped work best.

Try to find stones with a flat surface as they are easiest to paint.

Take the stones home and scrub them in the sink. Make sure you ask a grown-up to help with this part as stones can be dirty and grimy and not everyone likes to have dirt and grime in their sinks.

Once the stones are clean, let them dry completely. Be as patient as you can be.

You can draw your designs on a piece of paper while you're waiting for your stones to dry. Or if you're like Rowan you can skip the drawing and just go straight to painting.

Find some fairy paint or, if you can't find that, use acrylic or powder paint to decorate your stones. Acrylic is shinier, but powder paint washes off easily. (So if you like to change your mind a lot, use powder paint.)

You can decorate your stones with patterns or stripes. You can cover your stone with just one colour. Or you can write messages on your stones. Here are some Valentine's messages that could fit on a stone:

XOXO
BE MINE
U R CUTE
LUV U

Sometimes fairies write messages and leave them for children to find. Be on

the lookout for fairy stones – someday
there may be a message waiting for you.

Read on for a
sneak peek of...

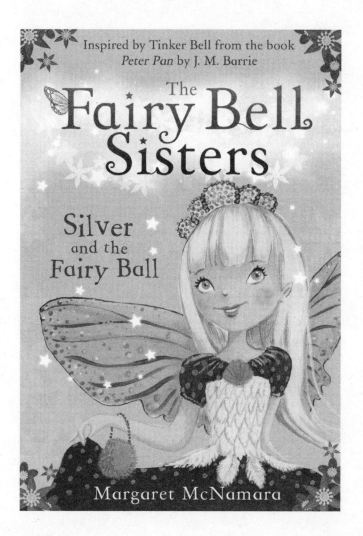

Inspired by Tinker Bell from the book
Peter Pan by J. M. Barrie

The
Fairy Bell
Sisters

Silver
and the
Fairy Ball

Margaret McNamara

 Chapter One

*E*verybody has heard of the Fairy Ball on Sheepskerry Island, for it's the only ball where fairies put on their diamond wings and walk on satin ribbons under the stars. But only a few of us will ever see those diamonds or find those ribbons. This is what they look like, just so you'll know when you do see them.

And though this is quite a secret, I'll tell you something as long as you promise not to tell anyone else: this year's ball was nearly ruined. And it would have been, except for one of Tinker Bell's little sisters.

Oh yes, of *course* Tinker Bell has little sisters. Tink is a grown-up fairy, so she lives on the island of Never Land with her friend Peter Pan. Some people think Tink's entire family lives in Kensington Gardens in London, as that's where Tink was born, but that's not true at all. Her sisters aren't grown up yet, so their home is with the younger fairies on Sheepskerry Island, which I believe is not far from where you are right now.

You may have been there without even knowing it, as on maps used by grown-up people it goes by another name. But perhaps you'll recognise it if I describe it to you. It's a jewel of a place, bright green in spring, silent white in winter, and filled with sturdy yellow roses in summer and flaming leaves in autumn. And it holds all manner of secret things that you will know about very soon. If you read the next chapter, that is.

To be continued…